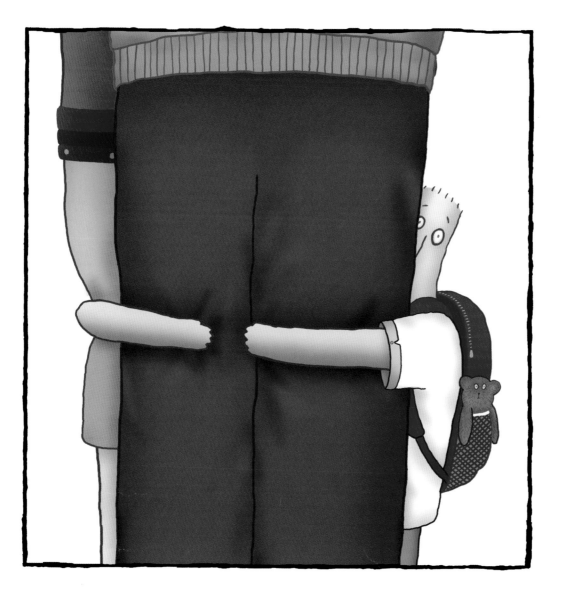

For great teachers everywhere,
especially my sister,
Ellen.

SQUARE
FISH

An Imprint of Macmillan

JAKE STARTS SCHOOL. Copyright © 2008 by Michael Wright. All rights reserved.
Distributed in Canada by H.B. Fenn and Company, Ltd.
Printed in April 2010 in China by Leo Paper, Heshan City, Guangdong Province.
For information, address Square Fish, 175 Fifth Avenue, New York, NY 10010.

Square Fish and the Square Fish logo are trademarks of Macmillan and
are used by Feiwel and Friends under license from Macmillan.

Library of Congress Cataloging-in-Publication Data Available
ISBN: 978-0-312-60884-2

Originally published in the United States by Feiwel and Friends
Square Fish logo designed by Filomena Tuosto
The text type is set in 32-point Hank
First Square Fish Edition: 2010
Book design by Rich Deas
10 9 8 7 6 5 4 3 2 1
www.squarefishbooks.com

JAKE

STARTS SCHOOL

By Michael Wright

SQUARE FISH

FEIWEL AND FRIENDS
NEW YORK

Jake woke up his first day of school
as sunshine filled the sky,
and Fred, his dog, jumped on his bed,
then licked him in the eye.

Jake brushed
his teeth,
he combed his hair,
he wore his
favorite shirt.

And packed inside his
lunch box were
two cookies for dessert.

When Mom and Dad called,
"Time to go!"
they drove off in the van,
to Jake's first fun-filled day of scho

..at least that was the plan.

As they arrived, Jake was surprised to see so many kids.

Some of them he'd seen before, but most he never did.

Then there it was, Room Number 1,
where Jake would join his class.
It looked so big, he felt so small,
he passed a little gas.

Just then, the door swung open and a red-haired lady said…

Jake screamed, and then he fled.

He grabbed his parents at the knees
and would not let them go.
They told him "Please, we have to leave,"
but all he'd say was "NO!"

His teacher tried to pry him off,
the principal did, too.
The school nurse gave it her best shot
until her face turned blue.

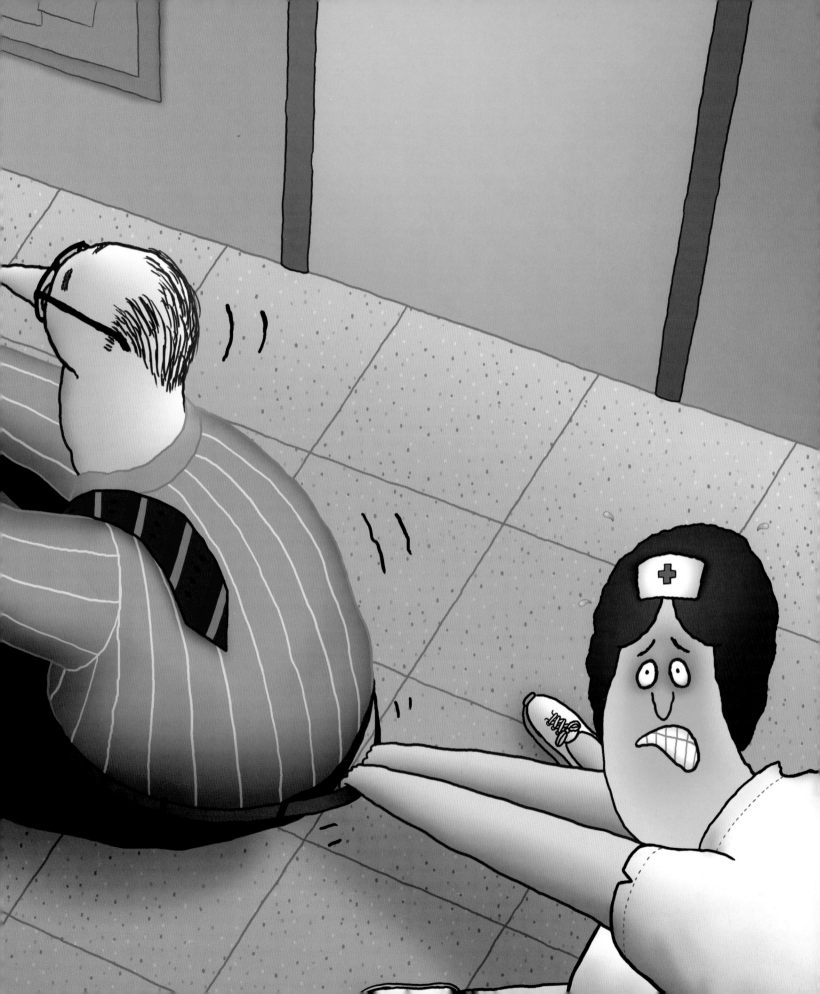

"There is no choice," his teacher's voice said to the clumping mass. "It's looking like the three of you will have to come to class."

They walked into the room as one
and tried to be discreet.
But that's not easy when you've got
three people in a seat.

Jake could not do a single thing
as long as he held on.
No playing with the other kids,
no joining in a song.

RYAN

JAKE

GLUE

AMANDA

GLUE

Finger painting was no fun
without a hand or two.
His clay would stay a blob all day,
he could not squirt the glue.

GLUE

DARNEL

They tried to take a seesaw ride
but didn't have much fun.

It's just no good when one side's light
and the other weighs a ton.

The tricycles were terrible,

so was the jungle gym.

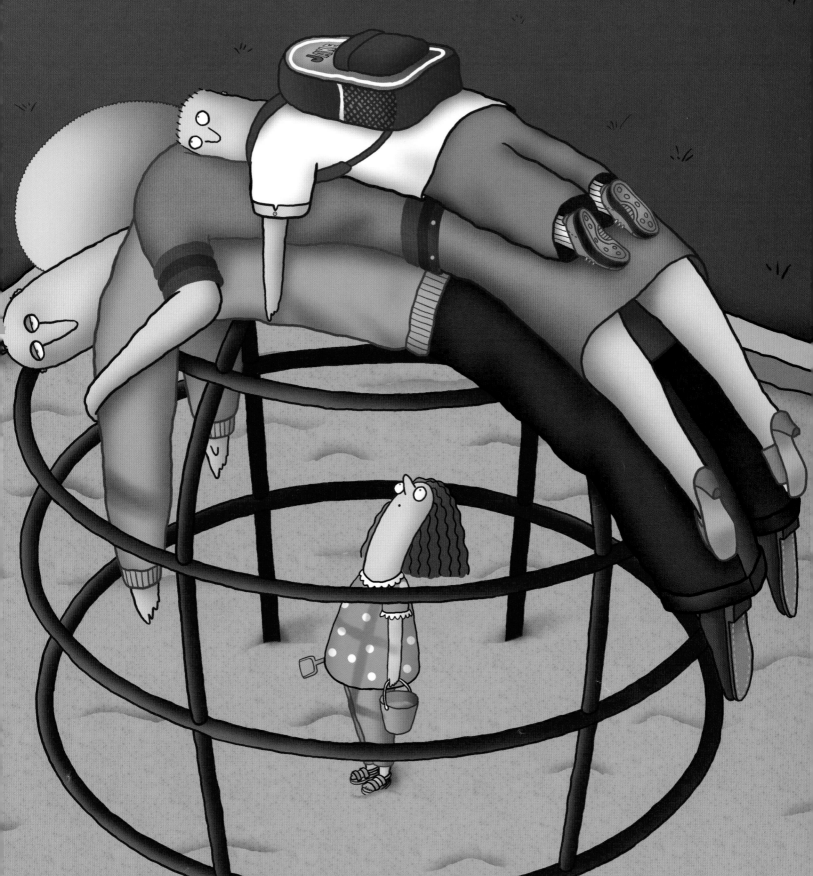

He could not take
a bathroom break.
He had to hold it in.

He could not feed the classroom pets,
the turtle or the bird.
There was no way to make a friend.
He didn't speak a word.

His teacher finally told the class
that soon the bell would ring
and school would let out for the day.
But there was
"One more thing....

I'd like
to read a story before
our day is through.
So everybody take your place, and
I will read to you.

She turned and reached
up on the shelf
and found
one special book.

Pumpkin

Peas

Squash

The Cow That Flew To Miami

Timmy Ties His Shoes

A Friend for Gwendolin

ABC's

My Pants Itch!

THE REALLY THICK BOOK OF DINOSAURS

INVENTORS

Planets

ATLAS

LOST in the Louvre

Rainy Day Stories

I Can Count! 678910 12345

Fairy Tales & Nursery Rhymes

my dog Fred

STAYS AWAKE

Bug in yo backy

This one's about
a dog named Fred.
Why don't we take
a look?

Then from the back part of the room,
there came a tiny sound.

His teacher grinned and asked,

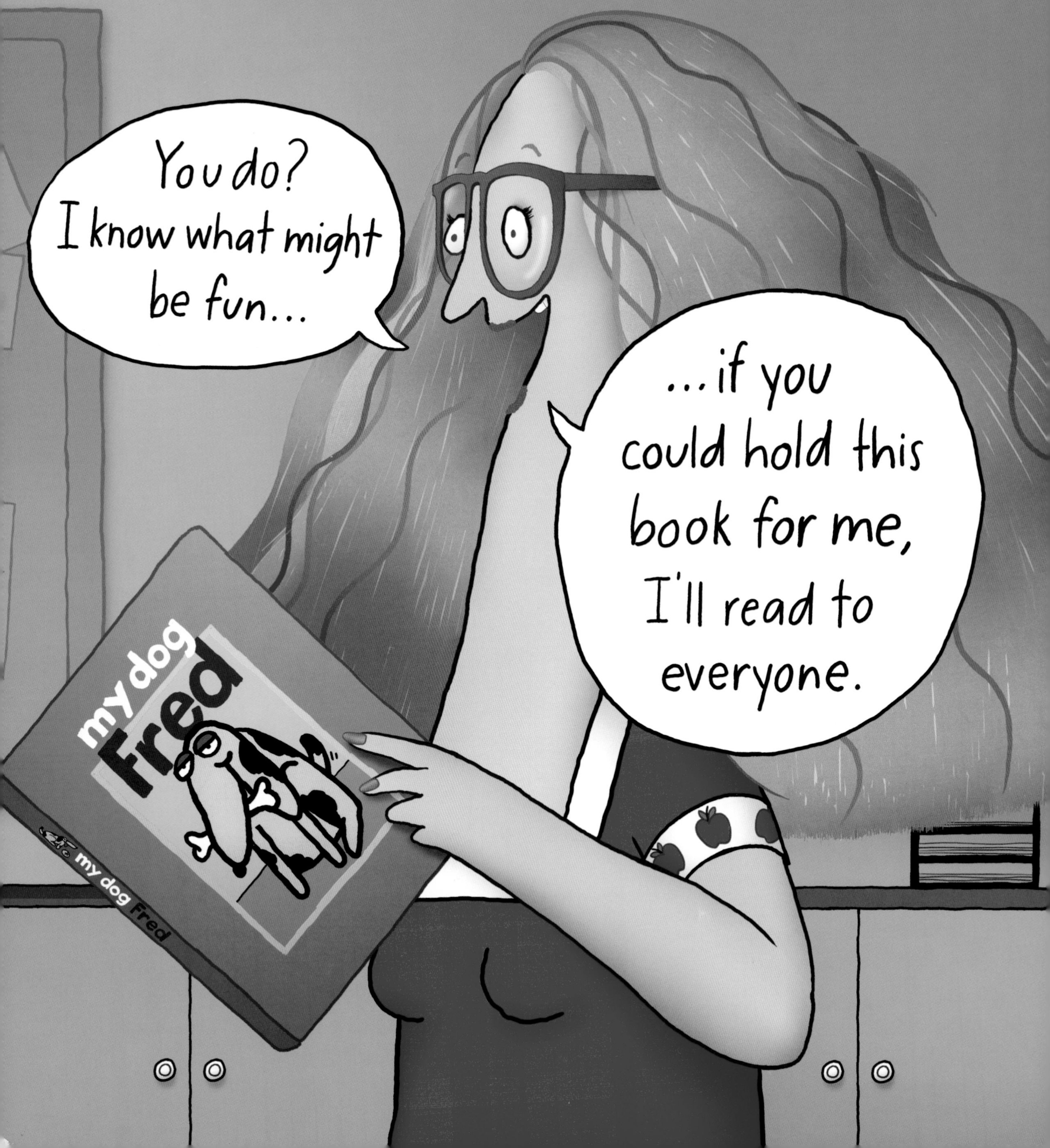

That's when Jake let his parents go,
and they felt some relief.
It'd been a while since they had
some feeling in their feet.

With every page, Jake loosened up,
and saw from where he stood,
the whole class sat and smiled at him.
And inside, he felt good.

Fred
wants
to play
now.

And when the closing bell rang out,
Jake looked to Mrs. Moore.
And gave her his last cookie
as he walked right out the door.

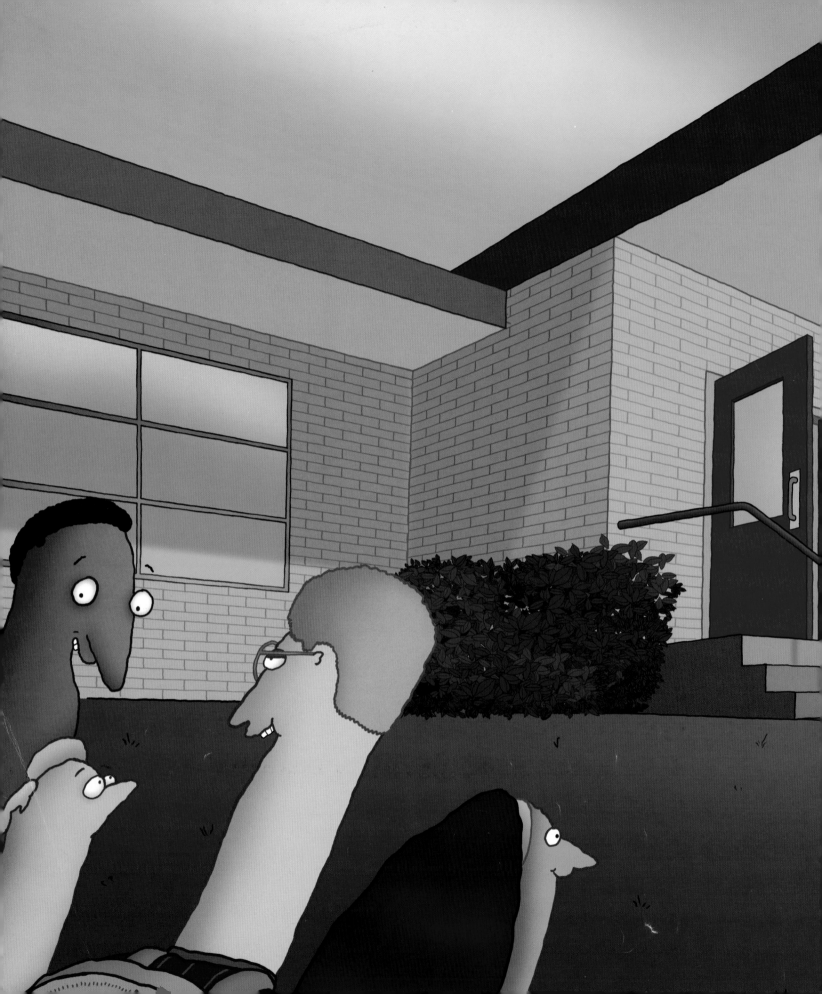

This whole first year with Mrs. Moore
has been a lot of fun.
Jake's special place to learn and grow
is classroom Number 1.